The Adventures of Chi-Chi the Chinchilla and the Three Worlds

Ekaterina Gaidouk

ISBN: 978-1-4834-3010-2 (sc)
ISBN: 978-1-4834-3011-9 (e)

Lulu Publishing Services rev. date: 5/12/2015

To the Children and to those who are Children at Heart

Already well known for his adventures and fun, Chi-Chi the chinchilla continued to tell his tales of Piola. He became even more popular after his last adventure. Chi-Chi of course enjoyed the attention from all the chinchillas and did not hesitate to retell his tale over and over again!

What he didn't know was that a new adventure was about to begin . . .

"Chi-Chi, tell us again how you got stuck in the tree trunk," asked one of the chinchillas as they formed their usual circle around the cheerful chinchilla.

"Hahaha gladly, but another time—I promised my dad I would go pick up some tree twigs by the Great Lake."

His best friend Ponchik tagged along as they left their circle of friends to go pick up the tree twigs that chinchillas used to build their homes.

They started on their usual trail that led to the Great Lake where they picked the tree twigs that fell from trees nearby. All of a sudden, Chi-Chi came upon a purple tail!

"Ponchik look! This must be some sort of weird animal. I have never seen a color like that!"

Chinchillas are all about exploration but this color was quite unique and as Chi-Chi stepped closer and closer—he decided to pull it!

“Hey . . . What do you think you are doing!?” asked a purple chinchilla as she jumped out of the bushes. “Let go of my tail!”

She was purple, a bit assertive, and Chi-Chi immediately did not like her.

“What do you think you are doing pulling on my tail?” she asked Chi-Chi. “And what are you staring at?” she asked Ponchik.

Ponchik and Chi-Chi were both speechless since they had never seen a purple chinchilla before.

“If both of you are just going to stand there staring you might as well help me. I need to get home and I'm trying to find a way to fix my raft,” she said pointing at the raft that seemed to be falling to pieces in the lake.

“I'll help you!” said Ponchik eagerly. He was immediately charmed by the purple chinchilla and wanted to prove himself. Clumsily he jumped onto the wooden raft but as he did so, the strings that were keeping the raft together came apart and the whole raft broke apart sinking.

“No, no, no . . .” cried the purple Chinchilla. “Now my raft is broken. How am I supposed to get home to Mimi Village?”

“How was I supposed to know it would break?” asked Pochik as he clumsily climbed out of the water. They all looked at the raft separating and drifting into the water. The purple Chinchilla looked at Chi-Chi and Ponchik with tears in her eyes.

Great, she is crying now . . . thought Chi-Chi, annoyed and giving Ponchik an angry look. "Why don't you come back to our village until we can figure a way home for you?"

Chi-Chi had never heard of Mimi and had no way to offer a solution. But he thought it would be best if she came back with them. "What is your name?"

"My name is Chilla. My village is pretty far away so yes I suppose it is best if I come with you two," answered Chilla hesitantly.

As they began to walk, Chi-Chi asked, "Where exactly are you from? I have never seen a color coat like yours before."

"My village, Mimi, is far away across the Great Lake. All the chins (short name for chinchillas) that live there have different color fur coats, pink, blue, purple, any color really . . . actually yours is a coat that I have never seen and so is your round friend's over there. Also, I wouldn't go around pulling other animal's tails," said Chilla defensively.

"Okay, sorry about that . . . so you are from Mimi. I'm sure once we get back to my home my parents can tell us the best way for you to get back."

As they walked on and arrived at Chi-Chi's village, Chilla noticed something unusual ....all the chinchillas they passed had dark or grey fur coats!

Finally, they arrived at Chi-Chi's home, and Chi-Chi introduced her to his parents. "Mom, Dad, this is Chilla; she is from Mimi. Ponchik broke her raft and she has no way to get back home."

"Oh dear, are you okay? My, what a beautiful fur coat you have!" said Chi-Chi's mother. "Ponchik, why don't you go home and we will have Chilla stay with us and join you in school tomorrow until we figure something out."

"It's almost morning. C'mon you two, let's have dinner and off to bed you go," said Chi-Chi's mom. Chinchillas are nocturnal animals so they sleep only during the early hours of the day. "Chilla, we will make you a bed on our couch."

As they sat around the table Chi-Chi's parents kept asking Chilla questions—not giving Chi-Chi his usual attention. Chi-Chi immediately felt even more annoyed.

The next day, right after noon, Chi-Chi and Chilla both went off to school together. Although they went to different classes, all Chi-Chi could hear at the end of the day was "Chilla, Chilla, Chilla" and "her amazing purple coat."

It seemed everyone forgot about Chi-Chi's adventures and just wanted to focus on Chilla and her fur coat. *Gosh*, Chi-Chi thought, *I have to somehow help Chilla get home. This is becoming ridiculous: "Chilla this and Chilla that."*

Several days passed and Chilla's popularity grew. Instead of hearing Chi-Chi's stories, now all the chins wanted to hear Chilla's stories.

Okay, enough of this, Chi-Chi thought. *I have to help her get home.*

As they were sitting around the dinner table, Chi-Chi's mom asked, "How was the day, you two? Anything exciting happen?"

"Not really. I really like it here, but I do miss home," answered Chilla.

"I know, honey; Chi-Chi's dad and I are trying to figure out the best way for you to get back. But we do not cross the Great Lake or have rafts, so right now we just have to be patient."

"There is a way, dear," said Chi-Chi's father, "but it would require Chilla to go through three different forests; each is almost like its own world . . ."

'I can go with her!" Chi-Chi said, jumping up. "I mean, I would love to help Chilla get back home."

"But son, it is pretty far away and neither I nor your mother have much to offer you in the way of directions except the hints that have been passed down from generation to generation . . ."

"Daaad, but I have gone through a portion of the forest before and I know I can take Chilla home!" said Chi-Chi confidently.

"Yes please! Can we go?" asked Chilla.

"Yes can we?" asked Chi-Chi.

"I'll allow this trip if you two stick together. The journey is long and the three different worlds through the forests are difficult to get through. All I can give you are these hints, but you two have to stick together—two heads are better than one!"

"Yes, yes we will," said Chi-Chi hurriedly.

"Chi-Chi, Chilla, the three worlds you must pass through to get to Mimi are unique; they will challenge you, but you must think of how to get through them—remember, there is always a way. Here is a poem with hints to help you understand the journey better," said Chi-Chi's father as he took out and read what looked like an old scroll:

The three worlds are not easy to get through;

The first is the opposite of what you are used to.

The second world is full of riches but be careful, for if you do
not have enough it will surely make it tough!

The third world is that of black and white, refusing to see the gray, middle side.

All these worlds you can pass, just think differently from that which surrounds
you and the worlds will open up as if there is nothing that binds them.

The things you will receive from each will not make you rich, but if combined
they can build what you really need, essentially, a bridge.

"This is all I can give you as far as the hints go because this was given to me by my father and I myself have never been to Mimi, but I do hear it is quite beautiful and colorful!"

"Hmm, interesting but I'm sure it's not as tough as my last adventure," said Chi-Chi proudly.

Chilla rolled her eyes. "Right."

"Chilla, I've been to Piola, I'm sure I can get you to Mimi." Chilla rolled her eyes again.

"Chilla, Chi-Chi, you must work together and travel together," interrupted Chi-Chi's mother sternly.

"Yes we will," said both Chi-Chi and Chilla.

Chi-Chi's father handed Chi-Chi the hints. "You two should probably leave first thing tomorrow."

THE THREE WORLDS ARE NOT EASY TO GET THROUGH
THE FIRST IS THE OPPOSITE OF WHAT YOU ARE USED TO.
THE SECOND WORLD IS FULL OF RICHES
BUT BE CAREFUL, FOR IF YOU DO NOT HAVE ENOUGH IT
WILL SURELY MAKE IT TOUGH!
THE THIRD WORLD IS THAT OF BLACK AND WHITE,
REFUSING TO SEE THE GRAY, MIDDLE SIDE.
ALL THESE WORLDS YOU CAN PASS,
JUST THINK DIFFERENTLY FROM WHICH THAT
AND THE WORLDS WILL OPEN UP AS IF THERE
YOU WILL RECEIVE
THEY

Next day, after hugging his parents, Chi-Chi and Chilla set off on their journey.

"We should go West," said Chi-Chi as they set out

"You mean East," Chilla countered.

"West."

"East."

"West! Look Chilla, I'm holding the map, so I will be the one giving directions," said Chi-Chi.

"The map is upside down. . ." Chilla said, turning the map over. "We go East."

Annoyed, Chi-Chi agreed and they went East.

They walked and walked and walked some more to their first destination, the World of Opposite, Olo.

"Ugh. I'm tired. Let's just sit down—seems like we have been walking for hours and I still have not seen anything opposite," said Chilla.

"All right, I agree. I thought we would be closer to Olo by now." Chi-Chi sat on a rock and Chilla sat next to him. He took out a couple of raisins and shared them with her.

"We were supposed to be there already and I do not see anything opposite," said Chi-Chi.

"Well, that's pretty opposite," said Chilla. "Look!" She pointed to a bunch of fish that started jumping out of the water and flying! They used their fins to fly above Chi-Chi and Chilla. "Whoa!"

They got up and kept on walking. As they walked on they realized slowly that things did seem opposite—trees were upside down, apples and other fruits grew on the ground and they could not find a way out of the forest.

"Chi-Chi, how are we going to get to the next world?" asked Chilla. "We seem to just be walking on and on."

Chi-Chi had to agree: there was no clear path, trees were upside down blocking their view, and they had no directions or anything to help them. The map he had only led him to the entrance without many details. They needed help because, like the poem had said, everything seemed to be the opposite of what they were used to. The only clear space was the sky above the lake.

"We will have to ask for a ride above the forest," said Chi-Chi.

"How? From whom?" asked Chilla.

"From a bird. I'm sure they can help give us a lift. Especially if we come upon two!"

"Okay, sounds like a plan." They kept on walking and looking for birds but all they saw were flying fish.

"Hmmm," said Chilla. "Let's go to the water."

"But Chilla, the birds will be somewhere away from the water."

"Chi-Chi, we have walked around the trees for hours now. I have not seen one bird—have you?"

"No," agreed Chi-Chi.

"All right, let's go to the water; this is the World of Opposite . . ."

As they came to the lake they found huge flamingos!

Chi-Chi and Chilla hurriedly ran to the water and jumped on a rock and called the flamingos over.

"Excuse me, Mr. Flamingo. My name is Chi-Chi and this is my friend Chilla. We need help getting to the village of Portika, in the World of Abundance. Would you or any of your friends be able to give us a lift?"

"Sure but I'm not any faster than you on foot," said the closest flamingo.

"Not on foot, by flying!"

"Haha," laughed the flamingo looking over at his friends. "We do not fly; only fish fly."

"Wait, but that doesn't make sense, why don't you fly? You are a bird," said Chi-Chi.

"I'm a flamingo. My name is Harty, and it's always been like that; please don't insult me."

Soon other flamingos joined in and looked down on Chi-Chi and Chilla. "This is how it has always has been!" joined in the other flamingos.

“But that makes no sense,” said Chi-Chi getting frustrated. ”You are birds! Unless you are just too scared!”

“What insults, these chinchillas,” said the flamingos as they began to walk away.

“Chi-Chi . . .” said Chilla, trying to calm Chi-Chi down.

“But you are birds!” Chi-Chi said

“Hmm. This chinchilla is obviously dangerous; flying is risky and we could get hurt trying. He is out of his mind . . . Harty, let’s go!” said one of the other birds as they walked away.

“Harty, wait,” said Chilla.

“Chilla, it’s no use, they are just a bunch of scared flamingos, who don’t know what birds are supposed to do,” said Chi-Chi angrily.

“Chi-Chi, shush, we are in the World of Opposite. We have to respect their views.

“Harty, wait. Why do you have wings if you should not fly?” asked Chilla ignoring Chi-Chi’s comments. She decided to ask rather then tell these flamingos what they are supposed to do.

Harty turned around and answered. “Well I’m not sure. I guess it’s just the way we are.”

“Harty, it is because you are a bird and birds fly using their wings.”

“Hmm, I have always dreamt of flying but it’s just the way it is and always has been—fish fly and we walk and swim in the water.”

“Harty, how about you try? Look, there is a cliff; you can jump from it and it is surrounded by water. All you have to do is try because even if you fall, you fall into the water. C’mon, it’s just you and us,” asked Chilla, looking at Harty with her big eyes.

Harty felt a little sad for the chinchillas and couldn't resist Chilla's question. "Well all right," said Harty hesitantly. He did always dream of flying but was always scared to break the norm. *Hmmm, wings, okay*, thought Harty. *I can do this. If the small fish can do it why can't I? And they are using their fins!*

As they got up to the cliff, Chilla further encouraged Harty. "Look. Harty, just jump; you will be okay."

Harty looked down, closed his eyes, and jumped—with wings closed!

He fell straight down . . .

SPLASH!

"Harty, are you okay?" asked Chi-Chi, as he stood on the shore.

Harty's beak peeked out from the water, then his head, and then he fully emerged. Laughing! "Yes, yes, I'm fine," he said as he got out of the water. "Let's try again. That was fun!"

He kept on trying and trying. But he did not fly. Chilla encouraged him on top of the cliff and Chi-Chi made sure he was okay once he got out of the water.

"Look, Harty," said Chilla, imitating a bird. "Most birds fly with their chest forward and legs back. You are not even opening your wings."

"But I'm scared," said Harty.

"Harty, do you want to fly?"

"Yes, more than anything. Just like the fish," Harty said, smiling.

"Then just open your wings, push your heart forward, and jump. Even the fish with fins that look like wings fly only because they launch heart forward."

"Okay," said Harty. He flapped his wings, ran, pushed his heart forward, flapped his wings and . . . he began to fly!

"Wohhooo!" screamed Chi-Chi and Chilla.

"You see, all you had to do was leap with heart forward to fly!" said Chilla.

"I can't believe this. I'm flying," said Harty as he flew over his friends and back around the cliff.

As the other flamingos looked up and saw Harty flying, they immediately ran to the cliff and started to lose their fear, push their hearts forward and try.

One by one they all began to fly.

"This is amazing! Look at me! Wooo," filled the air as the flamingos swooshed around the chins.

“My friends, how can I ever repay you?” asked Harty as he landed in front of Chi-Chi and Chilla.

“Just take us to our next destination, to Portika, and we will be grateful.”

“Yes, of course but that doesn’t seem to be enough! Because you helped me lose my fear and fly, I will also give you this branch as a gift.”

“Alright, thanks . . .” said Chi-Chi as he took the branch from Harty.

“Don’t look so disappointed. You see this branch is the opposite of what it looks like: it’s unbreakable!”

“Yeah, right,” said Chi-Chi as he took the branch in his hands and tried to bend it, break it, and although it looked fragile and thin—it did not break!

“Hmm, let me see,” said Chilla. She took it and threw it against the ground and jumped on it. Nothing happened; the branch did not break.

“Hahaha, skeptical chinchillas. You see it is the opposite of what it looks like but maybe it will serve you on your journey.”

“This is an amazing gift,” said Chi-Chi as he took it from her and placed it into his book bag. “Thank you Harty!”

“You are welcome. Come on you two, hop on.”

Chi-Chi and Chilla climbed onto Harty’s back and he slowly ran, pushed his heart forward, flapped his wings and lifted off of the ground.

They flew over the Olo, the World of Opposite, realizing it was so vast they could never have crossed it on foot.

As they landed on the ground, they thanked Harty. "So Harty, what will you do now—since you can fly?"

"We will try flying South for the winter. Usually we had to make the journey on foot but now thanks to you we will make the journey early! Thank you, chins, you have made my dreams come true! Any time you need anything, know that Harty is here for you!" answered Harty as he flew away.

"Okay, should we keep moving?" asked Chi-Chi as the pair waved goodbye to Harty.

"Yes, let's go," said Chilla.

As they continued on they came upon piles of stuff everywhere! The piles were composed of everything from twigs to fruits and nuts.

Soon they noticed the piles were moving! Actually they were moving toward them.

“Hey watch it . . .” said a small round squirrel that was carrying a pile.

“What is going on here?” Chi-Chi asked, astounded.

“I’m not sure, Chi-Chi, but this stuff can fall on us!” said Chilla as they moved closer to each other. “This must be Portika, World of Abundance or Disorganization. Look at all this stuff around us—I can barely see a path,” said Chi-Chi.

The piles started forming a circle around them and they realized that each pile had a squirrel beneath it, holding it up!

“Who are you? What are you doing here? Are you here to steal our stuff?” questioned the greedy, round squirrels.

“No, no, please we are just passing through. You see, we need to get to the village of Blaso, the World of Black and White,” said Chilla.

“We need your help for we do not see a clear way due to all these piles nor do we have directions,” said Chi-Chi looking up at all the piles of stuff around him.

“Well, are you going to give us something?” asked the squirrel as he came up to Chilla. Chi-Chi defensively jumped in front of her and said, “You guys have enough stuff and we are just trying to find our way to Blaso

“Enough stuff?! Nobody has enough!” said the squirrels as they became noisier and moved in closer to Chi-Chi and Chilla.

DAD

"Hold on! Calm down! What is happening here?" said the fattest squirrel of them all. "Why have you all stopped collecting?" He was definitely the squirrel king; you could tell by his round belly, small arms, and a crown that was too small for his head that he took himself way too seriously and had had a little bit too many nuts to eat.

"I'm Nayr, Squirrel King of Portika! And have you come to give me a gift? What gifts have you for me?"

"Well sir, your highness I mean, we would just like to pass and we need the squirrels to move and show us a way out of here. Also if we can have shelter for the night that would be great," said Chi-Chi.

"Well, what do you have in exchange for what you ask? Twigs, food?"

"With all due respect it looks like you guys have enough stuff," answered Chi-Chi.

Again at the word *enough*, the squirrels began to shake and become rowdy and move with their piles as well as their tails. "They should leave, they do not belong, they have nothing to give us . . ." the squirrels said.

"Enough! We never have enough!" said the King. As he stomped his fat foot down, the squirrels followed and stomped their feet—all of a sudden all the piles came crashing down around the squirrels and onto the king himself!

The king became buried under the stuff!

All the squirrels started running around trying to collect their pieces, fighting over pieces, and unburying their items, but nobody was helping the king and nothing was getting done! Chilla tried screaming and shouting but nobody listened.

"Chi-Chi what are we going to do? They are not listening," she said.

"Hmm, well, we have to move the stuff off of the King. Let me throw the items over to you. There is not a way for me to do it alone. Let's just lead by example.

"I'll take that piece over there and throw it to you and you make small organized piles on the bottom."

"Okay, that works!" answered Chilla as she ran down and started catching the twigs, hay, and fruit Chi-Chi threw to her. Soon little piles of organized stuff came into being.

The squirrels who were scrambling around finally saw Chi-Chi's organized piles and decided to follow their example. Small lines and piles formed. Within minutes the king was free, and everything was organized without anything on the squirrels' backs. Everybody shared and nobody had to have a pile of stuff on their own back, they just took what they needed and added to each pile

Working together and sharing the items lessened the burden on everybody. The king was so happy he hugged both Chi-Chi and Chilla.

“I’m so happy I can just eat you!”

“Please don’t,” laughed Chi-Chi. “You see, it is a simple solution; if everyone works together you can achieve more and actually get the weight off everyone’s shoulders when everyone shares.”

“If you can help us find shelter for the early morning and point us in the right direction to Blaso, World of Right and Wrong, that will be enough.”

“Yes of course. Come this way and grab some fruit from these amazingly organized piles.” The squirrels were so happy they were dancing along the path. Chi-Chi and Chilla took some fruit and snacks and followed the fat squirrel. They could not help but smile at the celebration around them.

He led them to a small spot beneath the leaves and Chi-Chi and Chilla finally sat around and enjoyed fruit and dancing with Nayr, the king.

“Lamda lamba,” the song went and soon the other squirrels joined in. Now, as everyone knows, chinchillas are excellent dancers—well, so are squirrels.

So the king and Chi-Chi fell into a competition. They both turned, and jumped as the squirrels cheered them on. But as the squirrel king tried to twirl he fell and silence filled the air!

Chi-Chi helped him up and the king laughingly said, “C’mon everybody, what stopped the party!”

The squirrels joined in and Chi-Chi and Chilla danced the night away.

They did not fall asleep until the early hours but they huddled together smiling at their companionship.

By the afternoon they were on their way to Blaso, the World of Black and White. Since the piles were organized, when the king pointed Chi-Chi and Chilla in a specific direction it was easy to see the path.

Before they left, the squirrel king came up to Chi-Chi and Chilla and said, "Here take this, this small bottle contains drops of water that will multiply anything—until you say 'stop.' May it serve you in your journey as my thanks to you."

"Thank you," smiled both Chi-Chi and Chilla as they continued onto the road. Chilla took the string necklace on which the bottle of drops hung and placed it around her neck.

They continued on their journey and then came upon a forest with a clear path that seemed to be shaded dark on one side and light on the other.

The sun was setting and everything seemed to be one half of the other.

They walked along the path until they saw two huge spikey bushes blocking their way. They tried to walk around them but the bushes just followed them blocking their path.

Chi-Chi and Chilla were confused—no matter what they did the pointy bushes just continually blocked their way.

"Look Chi-Chi, you go right and I'll go left," said Chilla. "One, two three." They ran in opposite directions and the bushes split; two porcupines stopped each of the chinchillas in their tracks.

One porcupine had black needles and one had white needles. They stood directly on the path, blocking the way. Their needles would not allow Chi-Chi or Chilla to pass.

"Excuse us," said Chilla.

"Yes . . . ?" Both porcupines turned around. Their bodies seemed to be disproportionate to their heads, which Chi-Chi found funny, but he figured that laughing right now would probably not be a good idea considering the size of the porcupines.

"I'm Right," said the white porcupine on the right.

"And I'm Wrong," said the black porcupine on the left. "Welcome to Blaso. How can we help you?"

"We are just trying to pass. You see, we are heading to my home in Mimi, which should be right after Blaso. Can we please pass?" asked Chilla.

"This is the right path, dear, just take it straight," said Right porcupine.

"This is the wrong path, Right, hmm, what do you say?" said Wrong porcupine.

"Wrong, I'm Right"

"Right, you are wrong, this the wrong path."

"I'm right."

"No, I'm right."

"You are wrong."

"Yes, you are right"

"What?" said Chi-Chi and Chilla, confused.

The two porcupines continued arguing . . . blocking the path.

"This is not getting us anywhere," Chi-Chi said to Chilla. "They are completely lost in their argument, refusing to see the middle side . . . *think outside of the worlds.*" Chi-Chi remembered the hints his father told him as he stared at Right and Wrong arguing. "I got it! We must find a compromise for them to actually clear the way."

"Right, this is the wrong way because chinchillas can't swim and there is a river they must cross."

"Wrong, I'm right, this is the only path to their village." The two porcupines continued the argument.

"Guys, guys we are just trying to pass," said Chilla.

But the porcupines continued to argue.

Chi-Chi jumped in. "Neither of you is completely right or wrong.

"You see, to get home we must take this path, but it is not completely right for chinchillas because of the river on the path and since we cannot swim, we cannot cross it, so we must find a right path across the water!"

Right chimed in, "You can use the large leafs from the palm trees to float across . . . the river, the leaves are extremely strong."

"You are right and I'm wrong; they can take this path," said the Wrong porcupine sadly, starting to turn around and still blocking the way!

"Wrong, without your insight this would never have been the right path for us; we needed both of your views," said Chi-Chi.

Suddenly both Right and Wrong smiled and stepped aside, understanding that both of their views were needed to find and cross the correct path.

"Here you go, young chinchillas. This is a compass. It will point you in the direction to Mimi from anywhere," said Right as he handed the compass to Chi-Chi.

"Wrong, you were right, and Right, you knew Wrong was right, thank you both!" said Chi-Chi as he and Chilla walked on their way. Behind them they heard the argument resume between the two porcupines. "I guess some never agree in the middle," laughed Chilla.

They continued upon their path and came upon the river, with the large palm trees swaying above it. Chilla jumped on a rock and jumped upon the branch of a large leaf as it fell down on Chi-Chi. They both laughed and Chi-Chi helped carry it to the water and together they jumped onto it to float across the river. "We make a great team!" said Chi-Chi suddenly.

Chilla smiled and said, "I thought you didn't like me?"

"Haha, you are okay," said Chi-Chi, smiling.

They floated on the tree leaf across the river and reached the other side. They continued onto the path, with Chi-Chi helping Chilla unto the shore.

As they looked up, Chi-Chi realized they had finally reached Mimi, Chilla's village and home.

As they entered Mimi, Chi-Chi was the one who stood out now.

MIMI

"Chilla!" screamed a yellow chinchilla as she ran toward them. "Chilla is back!" said a blue chinchilla that popped out from the bushes.

All of a sudden Chi-Chi could hear "Chilla! Chilla!" all around him and suddenly he was surrounded by all different colors of chinchillas and he was the one who stood out!

Chilla finally saw her parents and ran to them.

"Ma, Pa, I'm so happy to see you!" said Chilla to her parents,

"Us too, honey," said Chilla's mother. "Us too. We searched for days and could not find you!"

"Ma, Pa, this is Chi-Chi. He is the one that helped me find my way home."

"Why, Chi-Chi come here!" said Chilla's father as he came over and hugged Chi-Chi and everybody joined.

Chilla laughed at the picture of Chi-Chi getting the attention that he so enjoyed. "It was nothing!" Chi-Chi said bashfully.

"Come on, son—this was a long journey. Come join us for dinner," said Chilla's father.

Chi-Chi joined Chilla and her family for dinner as they talked about the adventure. Chi-Chi looked around the family table and realized that differences were not bad but great. Differences made life colorful and interesting. Friends who are different can help you see things from a different angle—and that's a good thing.

Even though we are different, Chi-Chi thought about him and Chilla, *we are pretty much the same*. He sat back, looked around, and enjoyed a well-deserved dinner among the best of company.

In the morning, Chilla's parents came up to Chi-Chi. "Chi-Chi, we have a raft for you. It will take you home but it is not sturdy enough to go back and forth on. These rafts take us months to make but we as a village decided to give you one as a gift for bringing our Chilla home so that you can get home to your family."

"Thank you, I appreciate it!" said Chi-Chi gratefully but with a bit of sadness that he was leaving Chilla behind.

Chi-Chi packed up his book bag, gave everyone a hug, and walked out to the raft.

As he got on the raft, Chilla ran over and said, "Chi-Chi, here, take this. It is the gift from the squirrel king, but I want you to have it—as something to remember me by."

"But Chilla, this was yours and trust me, I'll remember you."

"No, it's okay, you can have it and thank you for everything," said Chilla as she hugged Chi-Chi and ran to her parents. They untied the rope and Chi-Chi was speechless as he floated away, realizing Chilla had become the friend he never had, the friend who would stick by him and also the friend who helped him go through all his adventures

MIMI

Toward the evening he got back home. He got off the raft and like Chilla's father had said it would, the raft broke apart.

Chi-Chi walked back to his home with all three gifts in his book bag. He reached his village and Ponchik and his friends greeted him. "Chi-Chi, Chi-Chi is back!"

"Tell us what happened? How was the journey through the three worlds?" they asked.

"It was longggg," laughed Chi-Chi. "I got these three items," he said as he revealed the three gifts: the unbreakable branch, the bottle of drops, and the compass. More chins started joining the conversation including his parents as they ran over and hugged him.

Chi-Chi spoke about his adventure and once again became the talk of the town.

N
E
S

His parents greeted him home with a cooked dinner. As he sat down to eat, Chi-Chi's mother noticed a bit of sadness in his eyes. "Is everything all right, Chi-Chi? You must be very tired."

"Yes, it's just . . ."

Chi-Chi did not want to say it but he missed Chilla.

"I'm just wondering if there is any other way to get to Mimi—apart from going through the three worlds?"

"Well, Chi-Chi, our towns have always been separated by the Great Lake. I'm afraid there is not."

"But maybe one day there can be. It is just water." said Chi-Chi's father with a gleam in his eye. "Nothing a bridge couldn't fix."

Next evening, chinchillas could not stop coming up to Chi-Chi and asking to look at all three items.

Even Chi-Chi got tired of all the attention and at sunfall he went over to the lake. He looked across and realized that Chilla should have been here with him telling the stories as well.

I must find a way . . . to get to her, he thought. He knew the flamingos had flown away for the season so he could not go through the three worlds again by himself; but his father said something about a bridge . . .

He looked at his three items . . . and remembered the hints. He took out the poem and read the last sentence: *"The things you will receive from each will not make you rich, but if combined they can build what you really need, essentially a bridge."*

That's it! I must combine the three items! . . . it will mean giving them up, thought Chi-Chi, *but what fun are stories and gifts if I cannot share them with the chin that was on the adventure with me?*

Okay, it's worth a shot . . .

He took the unbreakable twig, placed it on the ground, put the compass on it and dropped the few drops of water on it and said "Twigs, multiply by these drops of water until you reach Mimi. Compass will lead you that way. Since you are unbreakable, build a bridge that is unbreakable too!"

N
E
S
W

All of a sudden the twigs multiplied, grew in the direction of the compass, and formed a bridge!

Chi-Chi could not believe his eyes. Ponchik, who was following Chi-Chi, fell over. He called his friends and the village to come over. As Chi-Chi stepped onto the bridge, he could feel how sturdy it was.

He first walked and then ran across the bridge. Mid-way across he saw Chilla, trying to walk on the bridge surrounded by her village chins. Chi-Chi smiled at her.

The rest of Chilla's village followed her, and soon all the chinchillas, purple, gray, blue, yellow, and pink began to greet one another and rejoice!

Among all the commotion, Chilla came up to Chi-Chi and said, "Chi-Chi, where did this bridge come from?"

"I just gave up the three gifts to build it!" said Chi-Chi. "The hints reminded me that all I had to do was combine the gifts to build a bridge."

"But Chi-Chi, that means you lost the gifts!"

MIMI

“Chilla, the greatest gift I got on this journey was friendship, and that was worth building a bridge for,” smiled Chi-Chi.

“Me too Chi-Chi! Thank you and tell Ponchik he doesn’t have to worry about breaking any more rafts. I guess we don’t need any more adventures either now to get from one village to another.”

“Hahaha. Chilla, I’m sure another adventure is right around the corner.”

“. . . and I better be on it,” said Ponchik as he came up to Chi-Chi and Chilla and all three laughed as they walked across bridge.